MORTIMER

STORY · ROBERT MUNSCH
ART · MICHAEL MARTCHENKO

ANNICK PRESS LTD.
TORONTO • NEW YORK • VANCOUVER

©1985 Bob Munsch Enterprises Ltd. (text)
©1985 Michael Martchenko (art)
Original publication:
©1983 Bob Munsch Enterprises Ltd. (Annikin text)
©1983 Michael Martchenko (art)

Twenty-eighth printing, December 2004

Annick Press Ltd.

We acknowledge the support of the Canada Council for the Arts, the Ontario Arts
Council, and the Government of Canada through the Book Publishing Industry
Development Program (BPIDP) for our publishing activities.

Cataloging in Publication Data
    Munsch, Robert N., 1945–
      Mortimer

    (Munsch for kids)
    ISBN 0-920303-12-9 (bound) ISBN 0-920303-11-0 (pbk.)

    I. Martchenko, Michael. II. Title. III. Series:
    Munsch, Robert N., 1945– .Munsch for kids.

PS8576.U58M67 1985 jC813'.54 C84-099722-1
PZ7.M86Mo 1985

Distributed in Canada by: Published in the U.S.A. by Annick Press (U.S.) Ltd.
Firefly Books Ltd.   Distributed in the U.S.A. by:
66 Leek Crescent   Firefly Books (U.S.) Inc.
Richmond Hill, ON   P.O. Box 1338
L4B 1H1   Ellicott Station
                             Buffalo, NY 14205

Printed and bound in Canada by
Friesens, Altona, Manitoba

visit us at: www.annickpress.com

To Billy,
Sheila and
Kathleen
Cronin

One night Mortimer's mother
took him upstairs to go to bed—

thump thump thump thump thump thump.

When they got upstairs Mortimer's
mother opened the door to his room.

She threw him into bed and said,

"MORTIMER, BE QUIET."

Mortimer shook his head, yes.

The mother shut the door.
Then she went back down the stairs—
thump thump thump thump thump.

As soon as she got back downstairs
Mortimer sang,

Clang, clang, rattle-bing-bang
Gonna make my noise all day.
Clang, clang, rattle-bing-bang
Gonna make my noise all day.

Mortimer's father heard all that noise.
He came up the stairs—

thump thump thump thump thump thump.

He opened the door and yelled,

"MORTIMER, BE QUIET."

Mortimer shook his head, yes.

The father went back down the stairs—
thump thump thump thump thump.

As soon as he got to the bottom of the
stairs Mortimer sang,

Clang, clang, rattle-bing-bang
Gonna make my noise all day.
Clang, clang, rattle-bing-bang
Gonna make my noise all day.

All of Mortimer's seventeen brothers and sisters heard that noise, and they all came up the stairs—

thump thump thump thump thump thump.

They opened the door and yelled in a tremendous, loud voice,

"MORTIMER, BE QUIET."

Mortimer shook his head, yes.

The brothers and sisters shut the door and
went downstairs—
thump thump thump thump thump.

As soon as they got to the bottom of the
stairs Mortimer sang,

    Clang, clang, rattle-bing-bang
    Gonna make my noise all day.
    Clang, clang, rattle-bing-bang
    Gonna make my noise all day.

They got so upset that they called the police. Two policemen came and they walked very slowly up the stairs—

thump thump thump thump thump thump thump.

They opened the door and said in very deep, policemen-type voices,

"MORTIMER, BE QUIET."

The policemen shut the door and went back down the stairs—
thump thump thump thump thump.

As soon as they got to the bottom of the stairs Mortimer sang,

Clang, clang, rattle-bing-bang
Gonna make my noise all day.
Clang, clang, rattle-bing-bang
Gonna make my noise all day.

Well, downstairs no one knew what to do.
The mother got into a big fight with the policemen.
The father got into a big fight with the brothers and sisters.

Upstairs, Mortimer got so tired waiting for someone to come up that he fell asleep.

Other books in the Munsch for Kids series:

Many Munsch titles are available in French and/or Spanish. Please contact your favorite supplier.